The Creation

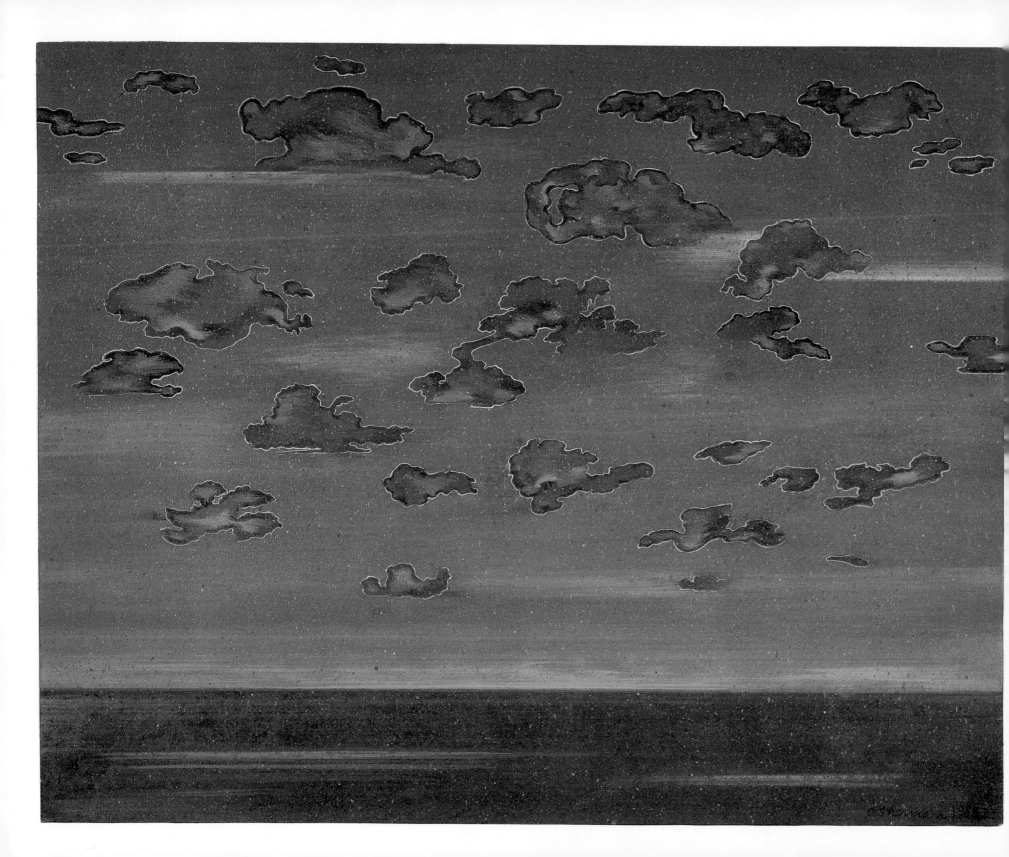

Paintings by ORI SHERMAN

The Creation

Translated and adapted by STEPHEN MITCHELL

 Dial Books New York

Published by Dial Books
A Division of Penguin Books USA Inc.
375 Hudson Street · New York, New York 10014

Text copyright © 1990 by Stephen Mitchell
Paintings copyright © 1990 by Ori Sherman
Printed in the U.S.A.
Design by Atha Tehon
First Edition
W
1 3 5 7 9 10 8 6 4 2

Library of Congress Cataloging in Publication Data
Mitchell, Stephen, 1943–
The creation / translated and adapted from the Hebrew Bible
by Stephen Mitchell ; paintings by Ori Sherman.
p.   cm.
ISBN 0-8037-0617-0.   ISBN 0-8037-0618-9 (lib. bdg.)
1. Creation — Biblical teaching.
2. Bible. O.T. Genesis I, 1–II,
3 — Illustrations.
I. Sherman, Ori. II. Title.
BS651.M56 1990   222'.1105209 — dc20   89-39726   CIP

EDITOR'S NOTE

The art for this book was created by a man who responded passionately and personally to the story
of the Creation. This is evident not only in the depth of feeling that radiates from the pictures, but in
the calligraphy included within the artwork. The artist makes use of *k'teev malay* ("full writing") —
a system of spelling that inserts additional letters to stand for vowels — though he occasionally uses
a more formal spelling. And it is not without irony that we note how on the final piece Ori Sherman
produced for this book, he has dropped a phrase from the transcription referring to God's period
of rest when the work of the Creation was completed. This painting was done at a point when
Mr. Sherman did not know how much longer he would be able to continue. In the words of Rabbi
Larry Pinsker, who served as Hebrew language consultant on this book, "Mr. Sherman strove to
complete the art before his death — rather than rest himself." What we are left with then is not an
example of formal Biblical orthography, but a glorious testament to the Creation story itself
and to the incredible vision it has inspired.

For my nieces, Leora, Rebecca, and Zoe

O·S

To Phyllis Clurman

S·M

In the beginning,
God created the heavens and the earth.

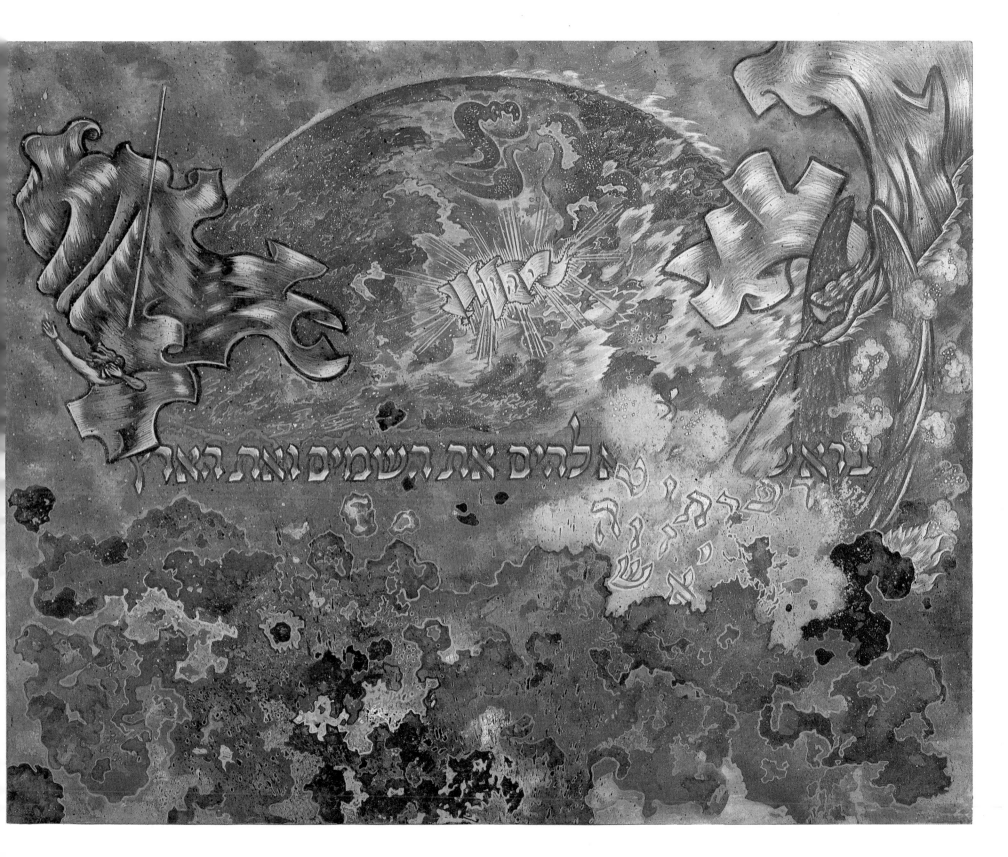

And the earth was chaos,
and there was darkness over the abyss,
and God's spirit moved
over the surface of the waters.

And God said,
"Let there be light."
And there was light.
And God saw that the light was good.
And God called the light *day,*
and the darkness *night.*
And evening came,
and morning came:
one day.

And God said,
"Let there be a sky
in the midst of the chaos.
And let the sky be above
and the ocean be below."
And God made the sky.
And God saw that it was good.
And God called the sky *heaven*.
And evening came,
and morning came:
the second day.

And God said,
"Let the waters be gathered
into one place,
and let the dry land appear."
And it was so.
And God called the land *earth*
and the gathering of waters *ocean*.
And God saw that it was good.

ויאמר אלהים יקוו המים
מתחת השמים אל מקום
אחד ותראה היבשה ויהי־כן:
ויקרא אלהים ליבשה ארץ
ולמקוה המים קרא ימים

וירא אלהים כי טוב:

O.Sherman 1987

And God said,
"Let the earth bring forth all kinds
of plants and grains
and fruit trees and flowers."
And the earth brought forth
plants, grains, fruit trees, flowers:
abundantly, according to God's word.
And God saw that it was good.
And evening came,
and morning came:
the third day.

And God said,
"Let there be lights in the sky
to separate day from night
and to give light to the earth,
and let them mark the
days and seasons and years."
And God made two great lights,
the sun to shine over the day,
and the moon to shine over the night,
and also the stars.
And God set them in the sky
to give light to the earth,
to brighten the day and night
and separate the light from the darkness.
And God saw that it was good.
And evening came,
and morning came:
the fourth day.

ויאמר אלהים
יהי מארת ברקיע
השמים להבדיל

בין היום
ובין הלילה
והיו לאתת ולמועדים ולימים
ושנים: והיו למארת ברקיע
השמים להאיר על הארץ ויהי כן:

ויעש את שני המארת
אלהים הגדלים את המאור
הגדל לממשלת היום
ואת המאור הקטן
לממשלת הלילה ואת
הכוכבים: ויתן אותם
אלהים ברקיע השמים
להאיר על הארץ: ולמשל
ביום ובלילה ולהבדיל בין
האור ובין החשך וירא
אלהים כי טוב:

ויהי
ערב
ויהי בקר
יום רביעי:

And God said,
"Let the waters bring forth all kinds
of living creatures,
fish to swim in the ocean,
birds to soar above the earth through the sky."
And God created great whales,
and the waters brought forth
fish that swim through the ocean
and birds that fly through the sky:
abundantly, according to God's word.
And God saw that it was good.
And God blessed them and said,
"Be fruitful and multiply,
and let there be multitudes of fish in the ocean
and multitudes of birds on the earth."
And evening came,
and morning came:
the fifth day.

ויאמר
אלהים

ישרצו המים
שרץ נפש חיה
ועוף יעופף על
הארץ על פני רקיע
השמים:ויברא אלהים את התנינם
הגדלים ואת כל נפש החיה הרמשת
אשר שרצו המים למינהם ואת כל
עוף כנף למינהו וירא אלהים כי
טוב: ויברך אתם אלהים לאמר
פרו ורבו ומלאו את המים בימים והעוף
ירב בארץ: ויהי ערב ויהי בקר
יום החמישי:

o.Sherman 1987

And God said,
"Let the earth bring forth all kinds
of animals, wild and tame,
mammals and reptiles and insects,
every kind of living creature."
And the earth brought forth
animals and reptiles and insects
and every kind of living creature:
abundantly, according to God's word.
And God saw that it was good.

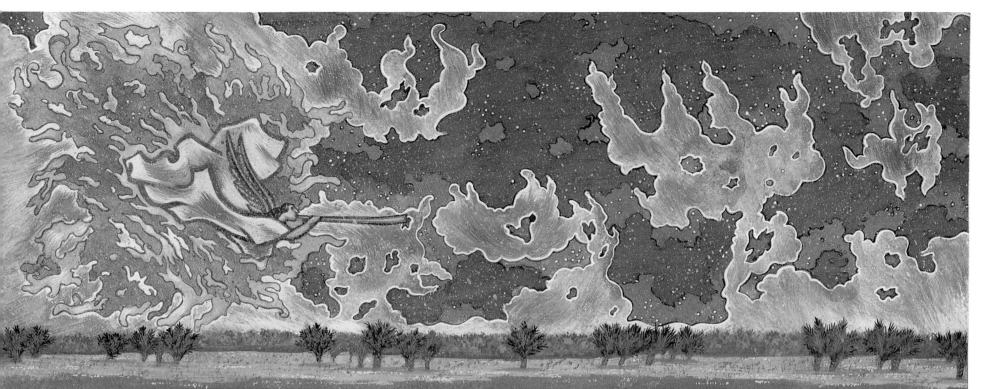

ויאמר אלהים תוצא
הארץ נפש חיה למינה
בהמה ורמש וחיתו ארץ למינה
ויהי כן: ויעש אלהים את חית
הארץ למינה ואת הבהמה למינה
ואת כל רמש האדמה למינהו
וירא אלהים כי טוב:

O.Sherman 1988

And God said,
"Now I will make human beings,
in my own image,
similar to me."
And God created human beings,
male and female,
in the image of God.

And God blessed them and said,
"Be fruitful and multiply
and fill the earth, and have power
over the fish and the birds and the animals
and over all the earth
and everything that lives upon it."

And God said,
"Behold: I have given you
every kind of plant on the earth
for you to eat,
every grain and every kind of fruit.
And I have given the plants as food
to all the animals
and to all the birds and fish
and to every creature on earth."
And God looked at everything in the world
and saw that it was very good.
And evening came,
and morning came:
the sixth day.

ויאמר אלהים
הנה נתתי לכם
את כל עשב
זרע זרע אשר
על פני כל הארץ
ואת כל העץ אשר בו
פרי עץ זרע זרע לכם
יהיה לאכלה: ולכל חית הארץ ולכל
עוף השמים ולכל רומש
על הארץ אשר בו נפש
חיה את כל ירק עשב לאכלה
ויהי כן: וירא אלהים
את כל אשר עשה והנה
טוב מאד ויהי ערב ויהי
בקר יום הששי:

So the heavens and the earth were finished,
and everything in them.
And on the seventh day
God completed the work of creation,
beholding it with great joy.
And God blessed the seventh day
and made it holy.
And in God's joy
was all the work of creation.

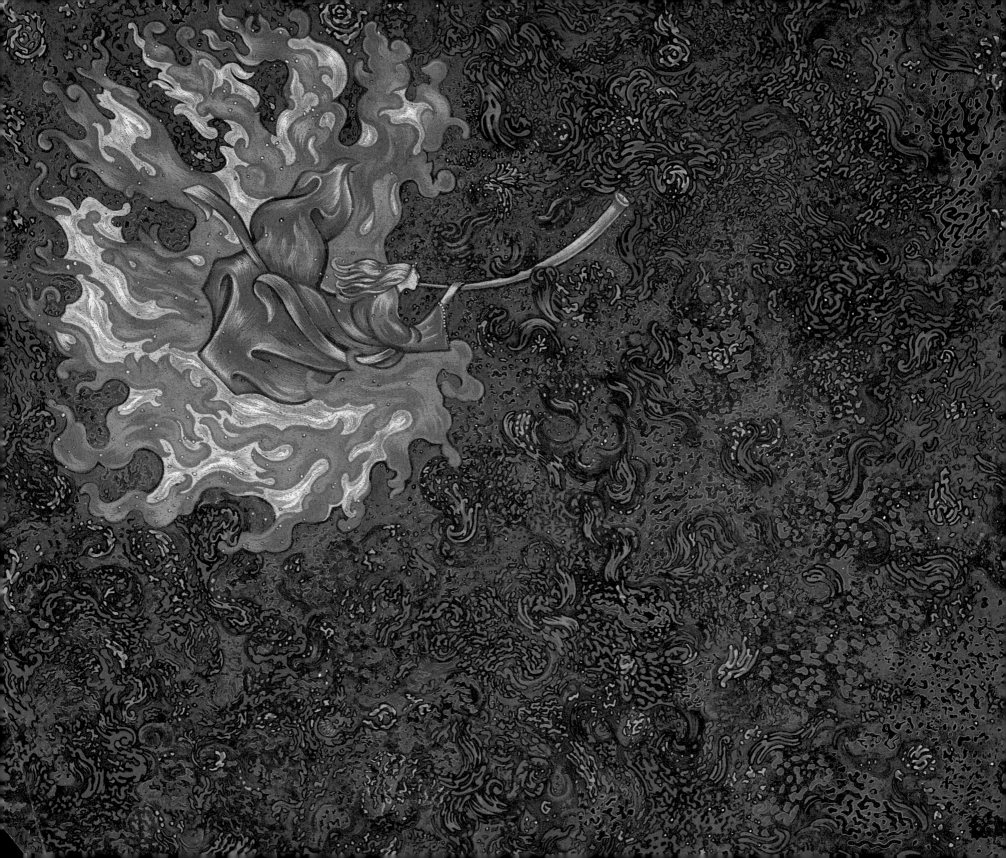